Clifford Chatterley

Virtual Encounters

Six Erotic Short Stories

AF198652

Virtual Encounters

Six Erotic Short Stories

Clifford Chatterley

Bibliographic information from the German National Library:

The German National Library lists this publication in the German National Bibliography; detailed bibliographical data can be found on the Internet at http://dnb.dnb.de.

© 2020 Clifford Chatterley

Production and Publishing: BoD – Books on Demand, Norderstedt

ISBN: 978-3-7519-2471-9

Contents

Foreword...7

Birds...9

Dream Come True..15

Roleplay...23

Tease and Denial...31

Pushing Limits..37

Acquaintances...43

Foreword

What is a virtual encounter? Given the variety of technological possibilities the dawn of the 21st century has created, this question is not easy to answer.

But this book does not linger over theory: Instead, it presents six examples in the form of erotic short stories that shed light on various forms and aspects of the topic.

Not all of them are technologically elaborated to the last detail. Some scenes may be considered speculative at the time of publication, some are only conceivable in virtual reality. Others are easy to imagine or can already be experienced today.

In any case, I hope you enjoy reading.

Clifford Chatterley

Birds

She was gliding calmly and steadily through the air, a few hundred yards above the coastal landscape below in the afternoon sun. An azure blue sea, a white beach that merged into a grassy dune landscape, a range of blueish hills further away. A little way ahead of her, gradually rising cliffs ascended from the sea, forming an imposing breakaway in the distance, much like the white chalk cliffs at the English Channel.

She felt the wind on her skin caused by her leisurely flight, the sun warmed her buttocks and back. It had been a while since her last trip to the Space. So she focused on becoming familiar again with the intuitive steering that controlled all of her movements. You didn't really need to know how it worked, mostly just by concentrating on a wish. She tried to climb a little, flew a gentle curve over the sea, sink a little and accelerate. Soon she gained confidence. She remembered, there were other perspectives, you could also observe yourself from the outside. She liked the naked avatar with the bronze-colored skin, the dark, flowing hair, when she set the viewpoint above and in front of her head, slightly offset to the side. Oops, that was close, she felt the environmental control make her climb a little to avoid hitting the gently sloping meadow leasing up the cliffs. Better slip back into the avatar.

She glided up along the cliffs, just a few feet above the ground, enjoyed the smell of the fresh green grass and the sea; screams of seabirds could be heard in the distance.

Once at the top of the cliff, she paused for a moment, peering over the edge down at the blue sea. As she considered, the intuitive motion control seemed to anticipate her request. She slid off the cliff at a slanting angle, accelerating towards the blue sea. A few meters from the surface of the water, she intuitively put her head back and raised her outstretched hands. The fall was intercepted, her belly almost brushed the surface of the water, she caught a few splashes of spray before rising again in an elongated arch, high above the cliffs in an external loop. She spread her arms and legs wide, enjoying the air on her skin, the warm sun on her stomach and thighs. At the apex, she effortlessly turned back to her prone position, softly intercepted the flight, and slid back over a wide arc to the edge of the cliff.

*

He lay idly in the tall grass near the breakaway, watching the woman who had just pulled an elegant loop from the cliff. With the zoom function, he had been able to easily determine that she was a woman. His avatar was also naked, as was the woman next to him, who had let another young man into her intimate distance. They were here together somehow, but it was not a possessive "together". The Space in which they were traveling had a few simple rules: nudity obligatory, only their own biological sex, and touching only with mutual consensus. He was still connected to his girlfriend, she replied his short "have fun" with a "good luck". English was the lingua franca in this international Space, but you didn't have to master more than these little phrases, it wasn't spoken. So he turned to the flying woman who was just approaching the cliff head again. "Cool stunt", he pinged. Like most of the other participants, he did not understand how the communication worked, it was not acoustic. "Invite." That was a signal word, he opened his intimate distance for her and waited to see what would happen. "Thanks", she replied, but the counter invitation did not come yet. As long as it was not given, the space would ensure that there was always a distance of six feet between them.

He stretched out as she slowly hovered over him, inspecting him. "Follow", she signaled to him. So he brought himself in flight position and followed her when she first made a slow lap across the abyss. He accelerated a little and hovered by her side. They exchanged looks. "Repeat." She dived, and he followed her plunging to the surface of the water. They caught the fall almost in parallel, their bodies bent in the G-force of the outer loop. At the apex they both almost came to a standstill. Suddenly the "invite" came back. He carefully approached her until his fingertips touched hers. He made a slight curve until they held each other's hands and looked into each other's eyes.

It was an important moment. You could fake almost anything here, you could tighten your face a little, but the expression could not be changed. Here the human behind the avatar shimmered through most openly. He liked her eyes, it seemed mutual, she smiled. They came closer, their foreheads touched briefly. Her eyes flashed, then she let go, pinged a "catch" while she was already scooting away. They chased each other for a few minutes in a high-spirited hunt, until she turned on her back in midair and made a rather quick stop with wide legs. When he landed halfway on top of her, she wrapped her legs around his back. "Lick", she signaled him, and "share control". That meant they would fly in sync as long as they touched each other. "Yield", he confirmed the request before attending to her open vagina.

*

She had not really considered what to do when she engaged with him. She had actually come to fly, to feel the wind in her hair, the G-forces, salt and water on the skin. But then, when the man had pinged her, she had answered without thinking twice. Now she was enjoying the gentle waves of excitement he gave her with his tongue as she spiraled higher and higher, just like a glider did in the upwind. She ran her hand gently through his hair, guided him a little, his hands securely on her hips, while she played a little with the pressure of her thighs. Finally, she released him from her leg scissors. "What next?" He smiled, turned on his back, his penis was already sticking out. "Yield", she handed over control to him, straddled him and bored the stake into her body. Leaning on his shoulders, she slowly rocked him as he held the circling ascending course she had started. She had no idea how high you could climb here, presumably that wasn't really limited, at least the world below was tiny. They didn't need the channel to each other, they looked into each other's eyes, played with each other's excitement until they simultaneously seemed to have the feeling "now".

*

He was still in control. Without letting go of her, he turned her around on her back, slid over her. He began to push her hard, but at the same time he tipped forward so that they went headlong into a dive he initiated. She was completely caught up in a series of intense orgasms as they raced faster and faster towards the open sea. Seconds before the immersion, he poured into her with powerful thrusts.

*

They must have let go of each other at some point after submerging. When she regained consciousness, she was lying supine just above the bottom of the sea. The Space had apparently prevented a collision with the sea floor and slowed her down gently. She felt his touch, he seemed to have reached the bottom not far from her. When he glided over her, she willingly let him in again, they made love to each other again, gently and persistently this time. Breathing under water was of course not a problem, both of them seemed to have been submerged in the Space before and could handle it well.

Finally, they let go of each other, heartbeat under control, breath normal. "Cool fuck, thanks", she signaled to him. "Good flight too." "Fare well." "Fare well." With that, he was gone with a few vigorous movements towards the water surface. She remained motionless for a while, letting the experience take effect while watching the small fish frolicking among the brightly colored corals. "Exit," she finally commanded. Her avatar was instantly gone.

Not a moment too soon: when she looked out of the kitchen window, she could already see the cloud of dust that followed the school bus on the gravel road winding up the Icelandic high valley to her farmhouse. In five minutes three children would storm in and loudly demand lunch, which luckily was already simmering in the oven. She quickly took off her gear, freshened up in the bathroom and slipped on jeans and a T-shirt.

*

He finally reached the surface of the water and with a few circles slowly returned to the place where he had left his girl alone with the young man. She was lying below the other man, but noticed him immediately. She reached out for his hand as he knelt beside her and gave her a hold, and she finally relaxed and let the boy's blows push her into a series of orgasms.

*

The young man who had poured himself into his girl was already gone. "Had fun too?", she asked. "Sure thing." He smiled. They had given each other mutual access to their records, and she could check every detail if she wanted to. "Gonna leave. Laterz", he said to her. "Laterz", she waved as he vanished with the "Exit" command.

Ten minutes later he was freshly showered and rode his E-Scooter towards the restaurant in Bangkok where he worked as cook. He was late, it would be a long night. He tried to remember the girl's home country. Austria? Australia? Did it matter?

Dream Come True

"You need not be afraid of the technology. But you need courage to face your own desires and fantasies." The woman looked at her frankly. The fine mesh already spanned over her head, the chip calibrated, the procedure had taken barely two minutes. "But take your time to prepare as it suits your imagination. Call me when you're ready." The woman left the room.

Anne looked around. There was no shortage of props here. While she was thinking, she undressed completely, she would not stay in everyday clothes anyway. She quickly went through the things that were available. "Very well, stockings. Black silk stockings. This is decided." She took a couple and took her time to pull them up over her long, shapely legs. She loved the feeling that only pure silk could create on her skin.

Next: delicate lingerie, openwork. A thong that concealed her most intimate place and yet displayed it obscenely. A bra through which her nipples were clearly visible. She stood in front of the mirror for a long time, then went to the dressing table. She knew her ways as a trained beautician, and soon she had exactly what she wanted: slutty, aesthetic but grotesquely exaggerated. Now into the red high heels, exactly matching her bright red lips. "Done", she said more to herself. The woman would notice, with the thing on her head.

The attendant was back ten seconds later. She nodded but said nothing. "That was 'no permanent damage, three minutes maximum loss of control'?", she asked business-like. "This is your first time here?" Anne consented impatiently. "May I advise you to take two minutes, it can be damn long." "Okay", Anne nodded, she was no longer listening properly. She had made up her mind and now she did not want to wait. "Good luck then", the woman said. "In there, you will intuitively figure out how to activate it. And remember, your safe code is an ice-cold shower." "I will remember, thank you." She sought her balance on the stilts and then resolutely went into the next room.

The robot sat motionless on a low stool. Anne took the time to inspect him, to touch his skin, his hair. It was amazing how real it all felt, even the fine hair on the skin. She stepped towards the wide bed behind her, lay comfortably on her back with her shoes on. Above her was a large mirror in which she would be able to watch if she wanted. Well then. She took another deep breath, then focused her awareness on the still lifeless man. Nothing for a few seconds, but then …

The man got up slowly, examined her. He was naked, Anne's eyes involuntarily slid to the middle of his body. The penis was not yet erect, but the flaccid size promised a lot. He walked slowly towards her. She remained passive when he touched her, enjoying the slight tingling that his hands triggered in exactly the right places. She closed her eyes for a while, feeling her sensations. Quickly she learned how to control his touches, how to strengthen or weaken them a little. Just lying to herself she did not manage: whatever she fancied, mercilessly became reality through the transfer to the robot. It wasn't even necessary to be explicitly aware of these desires, it was more like feeling that he was anticipating her wishes before she even became aware of them.

Anne took her time. She enjoyed him kneeling on the bed in front of her for a long time. He had taken off one of her shoes, he was sucking her toes through the stocking, while his hands gently caressed her leg, beyond the knee, but still at a safe distance to her most intimate area. She remained still, enjoying the tingling, the wetness that was slowly building up in her crotch. The man now devoted himself to her second leg with the same dedication.

She relaxed, watched herself for a while in the ceiling mirror, enjoyed how his tongue now slowly slid upwards her leg, licked it through the delicate fabric, slowly working his way up to the hem of the hold-up stocking, then slowly began to roll it down her leg. The touch of his tongue became more intense, she could feel the moisture of his saliva on her bare skin. Finally, he rolled the stocking all the way down and turned to her bare toes. The tingling in her private parts grew stronger, other, darker desires slowly pushed into her subconscious.

He let go of her toes. His grip became a little harder, more definite, as he took her legs in his hands and gently but firmly pressed outwards. Her body acknowledged this with another wave of lust that radiated from the center to the tips of her fingers and toes. Still kneeling, he bent down. His lips touched the little triangle of the string thong, which still covered her. A hand pushed it aside while his tongue touched her labia, gently at first but then more and more demanding, finally pushing them apart and penetrating them deeply. Anne involuntarily held

17

onto an iron bar at the head of the bed. The familiar sensations of the unusually deep cunnilingus mixed with surprising sensations. Small air bubbles? Tiny electrical voltages? She didn't really want to know. The man's head covered what she should have seen in the mirror, so she simply enjoyed the intensifying feelings. But the dark thoughts were already there, just waiting to break their way.

He stopped licking her and stood up. His expression changed from gentle and servile to hard and self-assured. He closed her legs and straddled her. His penis, already half erect, pressed hard against her stomach. He grabbed one of her arms, released her hand from the bar. She couldn't manage to resist when he tied the stocking tightly around her wrist. She had to swallow when he pulled the stocking and then wrapped it around her neck, once, twice. It took some tension to attach the other end to her second wrist. Her hands were close to her throat, the stocking pressed against the larynx, but she could still breathe freely.

He now attended to her bra. His hands gripped her nipples hard, and the silky soft fabric became surprisingly rough in his hands as he rubbed harder on her sensitive warts. She quickly learned not to reach out as every movement of her hands immediately increased the pressure on her larynx. So she let the waves of sweet pain roll through her body, while the feeling of unsatisfied pleasure took more and more possession of her mind. In the shade, her darkest, most secret imaginations rose. She still would not allow herself becoming aware of them.

The man suddenly stopped on her nipples. With a single powerful movement, he tore the bra in two, her bare breasts were suddenly in front of him, the sore nipples stiff. But he didn't touch her, he descended sideways from her with an elegant movement, his demanding hands slid down her body. She shivered with lust when they touched her prominent hips. Another quick jerk and the string was torn. He didn't bother to remove the parts entirely. He penetrated her quickly and easily with two fingers, his thumb played on her clit, exactly at that point, exactly up to that point ...

He let go of her again, let her soak in her lust what felt like an eternity. Then, with a firm, harsh grip, he pushed her legs wide apart, got on his knees, and penetrated deeply into her without any regard. Without touching her anywhere else, he pushed her slowly but deeply and hard. Apparently he could effortlessly keep his upper body in balance with the artificial muscles of his thighs alone. He looked at her with hard, unwavering eyes. She felt that there would be more to come.

Fear rose in her as she slowly realized her own dark desires, but her fear increased her lust at the same time. He waited, continuing the slow thrusts. There, something changed. Yes, it suddenly felt like her huge dildo, the one with the hard rubber nubs. Only that she had no control here. Music started. Monks who sang Gregorian chorals and the hall of a medieval Gothic church. The music grew louder, more and more dominated her consciousness over time, it was like a light trance. She adjusted to the constant pain that the knobs created in her vagina.

Yet there was more to come. He leaned over her, she felt his hard grip on her wrists. He looked at her, waited until she realized what the implication was, until her vagina contracted to a first slight orgasm. She took a deep breath at the crucial moment, then suddenly his weight rested on her wrists, which he relentlessly pushed further apart. She began to gasp, then cough, until she gave up fighting breathlessness and allowed her body to shake under him in violent spasms …

When her mind resumed, her breath was free again, but she was still panting heavily. The stocking was severed, the two halves still hanging from her wrists. Her vagina felt wet and sticky. She reached between her still wide legs and wet her fingers with the artificial liquid, which was deceptively similar to sperm. She licked her fingers, the smell and taste were familiar, wiped the rest on her stomach, where the liquid quickly cooled and created the typical sticky feeling.

The man was standing next to her. She looked up at him, his expression now attentive and respectful again. Her hand slid almost involuntarily between her legs. Even if he was good, at such moments she trusted only herself. She began to masturbate in front of him without any shame. He waited, one hand lightly on her stomach. When she was ready, he just put one of her nipples between the fingers of the other hand. She came violently again.

The man went back to his stool, sat down and suddenly froze again. She just stayed motionless for a long while, staring at her reflection on the ceiling. Finally, the woman came in, at that moment it didn't matter to Anne that she saw her the way she was: naked, used, one stocking still on her leg. "Are you okay?" She was holding a mug of water. "Thank you." Anne sat up, took the water and emptied the mug all at once.

"That was 45 seconds by the way", the woman said to Anne. "Even if it must have felt like ten minutes." Anne smiled. She knew it was only a matter of time before she would come back.

Roleplay

[04/23/2012 03:33] connected to server "Deutschlandchat" please respect our rules or be kicked.

[04/23/2012 03:35] entering room „Adult only"

betty28_RP: good morning.

Jana44: Good Morning betty28_RP.

betty28_RP: Ah someone wake here?

Jana44: and horny. Looking for roleplay?

betty28_RP: yes but I am f

Jana44: I know ;) Care playing with a woman?

betty28_RP: if you have time and an idea?

Jana44: Work starts at 8. Does this pass as having time?

betty28_RP: depends on your time to commute *fg*

Jana44: Touche. Do you have time?

betty28_RP: more than you. Currently unemployed.

Jana44: Aww. Single?

betty28_RP: does it matter?

Jana44: true. What whould you like to play?

betty28_RP: betty not Betty. Can you make something of it?

Jana44: taking you under the chin, lifting your head, forcing you to look into my eyes. Color?

betty28_RP: brown, sorry to disappoint. And black hair.
* Escaping your grip and lowering eyes *

Jana44: disappoint why? - care going somewhere else?

betty28_RP: thought it might. Where to?

Jana44: mom, hope I can manage

Jana44: [create room Magiccastle]

Jana44: [invite betty28_RP room Magiccastle]

betty28_RP: [follow Jan44 room Magiccastle]

***

[04/23/2017 03:48] entering room Magiccastle.

[04/23/2017 03:48] warning: private room.

betty28_RP: did it work out?

Jana44: looks like. Mind me making it a bit prettier here?

[04/23/2017   03:51]   new   background   image
sleepingbeauty_3.jpg

betty28_RP: wow cool what are you up to?

Jana44: Dunno yet. Figured a nice environment never hurts. What's your kinks sweet?

betty28_RP: sub. Well told stories with a lot of surroundings. Able to play along well. Some pain is OK but not as the main thing.

Jana44: dark hair? Are we going to make you a pretty sleeping beauty? You don't have to sleep 1000 years, an afternoon nap is enough as a start ;)

[04/23/2017 03:58] betty28_RP changing nick to sB19

sB19: smile. And you?

[04/23/2017 03:59] Jana44 changing nick to Joy25

Joy25: an extraordinarily handsome squire who comes to the castle on horseback to salvage you?

sB19: Squire?

sB19: Aaaaaah - some things need a bit of seeping: boots, trousers, jackets, a cheeky hat, come into the castle courtyard mounted on a white horse ...

Joy25: exactly. So I come to the castle courtyard one afternoon. Beauty is resting a little in the shadow of the ancient elm tree by the fountain – since she does not expect a visit, she is rather slightly curled.

Joy25: my devoted greeting, dear maiden.

sB19: my beautiful youth who are you, what leads you to this remote castle? Forgive my appearance, I did not expect a visit.

Joy25: Joy is my name, I was told that there was a lonely virgin to be salvaged from this castle. It seems to me that I am not entirely wrong here? Are you even the handsome Sleeping Beauty that is reported all over the country?

sB19: Sleeping Beauty I am, my beautiful youth, but I have stopped counting the brave squires who came here to salvage me. I still haven't figured out yet from what evil.

Joy25: Just say, you are not languishing here all day, longing for the one and only to salvage you and make you his wife?

sB19: And who then makes me breed a child every year and moves out again, to beguile other fair maids, while I stay alone in his yard and herd the growing flock? Thanks, my squire, but thanks no, I don't miss anything in comparison here. And if …

Joy25: And if - what, sweet maid? * gets off the horse and hands the reins to the groom who hurries over *

sB19: So if certain – feelings – should ever become overwhelming: it is rarely less than once a week I meet a squire like you here. But it is rare that this – desire – takes hold of me.

 Joy25: How so dear maid? * comes closer * what kind of a – squire – could take away your peace of mind? * gently reaches under your chin *

sB19: * shivers * seems is not always what the external appearance pretends to be? This finely cut face, the delicate hand, the grace of touch ...

Joy25: * smiles, then gives you a very delicate kiss, steps back, takes off the hat and shakes her long hair loose *

sB19: * gently puts both arms on your shoulders, snugly hugs * for a long time I had to do without what I longed for deep inside.

Joy25: * puts your hands on your hips, pulls you close * I'm Joy, but what's your real name, lovely child?

[04/23/2017 04:12] sB19 changing nick to aurora19

aurora19: * shivers a little * call me aurora if you will, beautiful Mistress

Joy25: aurora * kissing you again, one hand on your bottom while the other slides up your back *

aurora19: * shudders * maybe we want to freshen up at the nearby pond, Mistress? Your ride must have exhausted you, the water is pleasantly mild these days.

Joy25: * smile * so lead us to the pond you are so fond of, little aurora

[04/23/2017   04:09]   new   background   image pond_castle.jpg

aurora19: with your permission, Mistress. Follow me.

Joy25: it is wonderful. Will you help me take off my clothes, sweet little aurora?

aurora19: from the bottom of my heart, Joy * take your clothes piece by piece and put them properly in the meadow until you stand naked in front of me * Wow mistress, may I? * approach me gently and gently touch your lower belly with two fingers *

Joy25: wouldn't we freshen up first, or are you so much in need, sweetie? * take yourself under the chin and look into your eyes *

aurora19: * blushing * of course Mistress, forgive me. * quickly pulling my thin dress over my head, putting it in the meadow and slipping out of my panties. *

Joy25: * patting on your butt * come on then. * going ahead into the warm water * mmmh wonderful.

aurora19: * following you quickly into the water, swimming a little way out * follow me Mistress

27

Joy25: * swimming curiously as you disappear around a bend of the bank *

aurora19: * not too far away you can see a sunlit island that I'm heading for *

Joy25: * following, watching as you climb up the flat bank out of the water *

aurora19: * reaching out, helping you out of the water * welcome to treasure island * smile *

Joy25: * a little pat on your butt * you forget your manners, sweetie. But it's beautiful here

aurora19: * blushes * forgive me, Mistress. Do you want to follow me anyway, Mistress?

Joy25: * following you curiously *

aurora19: * after a short ascent we reach a small pavilion, the roof covered with wooden grids. A checkered shadow pattern falls on the wide freshly made bed in the pavilion *

[04/23/2017   04:32]   new   background   image pav_bed_2.jpg

Joy25: * smiling broadly * is it here where you spend lonely afternoons and is it here where you bring the prettiest of the squires, sweet?

aurora19: * blushing again * I would have to lie to you Mistress if I contradicted you. * Looking at the floor *

Joy25: * smile – approaching you, our naked bodies touch for the first time, skin to skin * an experienced girl has her special benefits, sweet

28

aurora19: * nestling against you * just like an experienced Mistress to guide me, Mistress

Joy25: * pinches you hard in the butt * then present yourself properly, as a little sub-bitch should know how to

aurora19: * turns red * yes Mistress. * kneeling on the bed, knees wide open, palms turned up on the thighs, eyes down *

Joy25: present your body

aurora19: Yes mistress * leaning back with my knees folded, arms behind my head on the bed *

[04/23/2017 04:47] Joy25 has left the room.

***

The man in his mid-fifties quickly closed the browser window and pulled his shorts back up when he heard his wife in the corridor. Seconds later she was in his room with him. She seemed to have grasped the situation immediately, but she only smiled smugly: "Ah, I see you are busy elsewhere. I'm going for another round of napping."

When he opened the chat again, aurora19 was already gone. Too bad.

***

"Fuck, she was good." The blonde woman, she might be 40, closed the chat app on her tablet. "Or him", her much younger friend noted, who was lying on the bed next to her and had apparently watched her typing the last few minutes. She sat up and shook her long dark hair. "Good morning, little bitch. You aren't looking for someone else now, are you?" She grinned. But the blonde woman was already kneeling wide on the bed, her palms on her thighs turned up. "Good morning, Mistress, at your service."

Tease and Denial

The Japanese-born in her mid-fourties was sitting naked in the shade of a mighty linden tree in the garden of her house near Düsseldorf. The fact that she was naked was of little consequence and was due to the fact that she wanted her body to be evenly tanned in the sun. She was wearing a headset, earphones and a microphone, and was holding a tablet computer in her hands. The job didn't bring much, only the active minutes were paid for, but it was much better than nothing, and where else could you tan in the garden at work and still live out your inclinations, at least in your imagination?

It was of course an advantage that she spoke three languages fluently, she could take calls in German, English and her mother tongue Japanese. The latter was more in demand than one would have assumed because the placement service operated in Western Europe and, for labor law reasons, only employed EU residents like her. Such barriers did not apply to customers, and the demand for cybersex in Japan, where much of the accessories supported by their service were manufactured, was high.

A call just came in again. Tokyo, it was probably late in the evening, she imagined a businessman who was alone in his capsule hotel and didn't want to just wank away his pressure for two minutes and then fall asleep on the Japanese commercial TV. Click. "Asuka, how can I help you?", she asked in perfect Japanese. The calls were displayed in pools, and whoever qualified took it first had it. "I'm Makoto, and I ask for your strict treatment, Mistress." She briefly glanced on the display. Full 3D helmet, stimulators for penis, testicles and buttocks, electrodes for the nipples. There was of course more, for more specific requests, but the equipment would go well. "30 minutes minimum, or would you like 60 for 50, Makoto?" "60 for 50, Mistress." She briefly checked his preferences: tease and denial, mild pain, humiliation. "Good choice, with or without a happy ending?" "With a happy ending, Mistress, if you allow so, but please make me wait for it." "Very well Makoto, charge was received, let's get started. Will you choose an avatar for me first?"

*

"Thank you, Mistress." Makoto was actually in his hotel room, but not in a capsule hotel, as a high manager of a car manufacturer he was entitled to a small single room. The air conditioning was running at full capacity and made the inside temperature more or less bearable. For a real woman, he would have had to go out into the heat of the night again, which did not seem attractive to him at over 30 degrees centigrade. Besides, he had special requests and here they would definitely be fulfilled. He leafed through the selection of avatars, finally got stuck with an Asian dominatrix with a hard look and wasp waist. He stared at "Select" with his eyes, it took a little while for the network to transmit the 3D environment, then he was in the middle of the scene. "Well you little pig, where are you hanging around again, does your wife know that you are here?" She stood at his side, her bare vagina inches before his eyes, but of course there was no way to touch her in the simulation. "And this is supposed to be a cock, don't you fancy me, it's not even really hard? Do you need some encouragement?" With her words, a stabbing pain shot through his testicles, he groaned. He felt the blood shoot into his penis, which finally filled his penis sleeve with the electrodes. "Well, you little pig. Does it make you horny to feel your balls well?" Another pulse of stabbing pain. "Yes, Mistress, thank you, Mistress", he groaned. The woman was good, that much was already certain for him.

*

She let go the scrotum of the small penis model that connected to her tablet. The simulation could also be operated entirely on the screen, but it was much easier with this little tool she had only bought a few months ago. The rest of the stimulation was not a problem on the touch screen. "When was the last time you fucked, and I mean really fucked like a man, Makoto?" She encompassed the penis model and began slow up and down movements. "Three days ago, Mistress." "And did you fuck your wife or were you on the wrong path, you little pig?" "On the wrong path, Mistress." She operated the "Slap" button on the display a few times. "Is that right, you little pig?" "No Mistress."

She didn't really have to concentrate anymore, after a few hundred calls like this, a lot was already automated, and she didn't need a watch to span an arc over 30 or 60 minutes, depending on what the customer paid. Experienced, she slowly began to jerk him off. Few customers knew there was a bio-feedback channel that assessed the "level of arousal" of the customer and displayed it on a scale from 0 to 100. However, 100 was

33

for the hard-boiled, for mild cases like this Makoto one could assume that he would ejaculate at 80 or 85. So she jerked him to 70, then stopped the movements and pinched him hard in the balls. "Awwww", he whined. "Well, that was one, you dirty little bastard, if you hold out until 60 I will maybe allow you to cum."

*

10 minutes. He already loved this woman. Apparently she had a natural feel for his "point of no return", her dirty talk excited him. He changed the perspective a little so that he could watch the avatar work his stiff penis with her mouth, fingers and nails, at times with gentle movements, then harder again. "Awwww," he moaned when she suddenly took him hard on one of his nipples. "Answer if spoken to, little pig."

He let himself go. The constant change of pleasure and pain and her softly spoken humiliating words had brought him into a kind of meditative flow, he was almost disappointed when she finally made him cum. She let go of his penis, stood next to him in the initial pose, her bare vagina inches from his eyes. He fixed the "Tip" button, he must have chosen the selection inaccurately: Even though she was good, he hadn't intended 2000 yen. "Thank you too, Makoto. I am Asuka, my preference code is 258." 258 he had to remember. There was no guarantee, of course, but you could give the code when signing in, and if the woman was online and free, you were connected directly.

*

She took off the headset. Paul, her much younger lover, had been standing next to her in the garden for a while, watching her at work. "Good evening, Mistress", he said politely now. She smiled at him. "Would your cock want out of its cage again? But be warned, I'm horny and in a very sadistic mood." He said nothing at first, but handed her a casket with needles and all sorts of other tools. "This is a good thing, Mistress, I have to confess to you unencumbered thoughts in your absence." She stood up and put the tablet down from her hand. "Unencumbered? Well then, on your knees and on foot", she ordered him. Paul obediently went on all fours and followed her into the house.

Pushing Limits

The special suit, which she had had made to measure, fit perfectly. Once you had oiled your whole body and put it on, you could hardly feel the ultra-thin, highly resistant material. The plugs in anus and vagina fit comfortably. On the whole inside, the suit was covered with a fine network of stimulators. She quickly got the two-minute functional check behind her. Now she put on the airtight helmet with the 3D visualization system, let her tongue slide into the opening of the mouthpiece. The air supply was connected via two thin hoses, then she was lifted into one of the large water pools. The salinity was automatically adjusted in a short time so that she was perfectly suspended, fine currents prevented a collision with the walls of the pool even when moving. She was turned a few more times so that she lost touch with real gravity.

*

The Space was an underwater world. She quickly got used to breathing normally. Morphing was allowed in this Space, which meant that players could change the shape of their avatar and thus the limits of their virtual body during their stay. At first, she kept her avatar as it was and explored this bizarre underwater world for a while. The rest of the Space rules still applied here, there was no contact with objects in the Space and none with other players without invitation. She tried swimming into a forest of creepers, but the plants dodged as if by magic, as if she was floating in an invisible capsule. With immovable objects, the space simply changed her course to avoid a collision.

But this was not why she was here. So she focused on the word "Level 3", and however it worked, a green arrow pointed down to the left. She followed the indicated direction until she saw a tunnel in a cliff at the bottom of the sea. It had to be the gateway, so she dived into the entrance. It was getting dark around her. "Level 3. Touch zone", the warning flared in red letters. "Accept." She was through the lock, a yellow "Escape to level 2, Exit to leave space" flashed up, she barely noticed it. The path led through a loose forest of sea grass, which clearly showed her the difference to level 2. She could clearly feel the touches on her whole body. Slight panic rose in her when she felt one of the plants wrap around her leg, but it was still easy to just focus on swimming. The "no constraint" rule still applied. She tried moving towards a narrow passage between two sharp-edged rocks, but she was pushed away.

OK, one more time. This time it worked. She had simply imagined herself to be long and thin, morphing had transformed her avatar accordingly. The outside view showed the bizarre shape she had just given herself. It was easy to reset the avatar to human shape. Better. She just let herself drift for a while. She was startled when unexpectedly something rough touched her from below. Ah, a fish. Touching, that was the kink that had brought her here. She had a phobia of being touched, especially unforeseen. But at the same time it was the only thing that aroused her sexually. The cold shiver that ran down her back slowly dissipated in a pull and tingling in her crotch. The fish was probably a bot, it did not further attempt contacting her.

Next, a fine bubbling in a distance caught her attention. She swam towards a cave from which fine bubbles rose. She waited, watching two other swimmers who had shaped themselves spherical before disappearing into the cave portal. She switched to the outside view and also tried to give her avatar a ball shape. It didn't work right away – concentrate. Ah, now. She slipped back into her avatar and dropped into the aperture of the cave.

Crazy, she thought, when she drifted again in the open water after maybe 15 or 20 seconds and still felt the tingling of the carbon dioxide bubbles on her skin. The way back was easy to find, she tried again. She was just feeling the gentle surge of excitement that had triggered it in her body when a "liked?" came from somewhere. "Yes", she replied. It was the little sphere right next to her. "Follow." The little ball floated away in a different direction. She followed curiously. Another cave apparently, there were no bubbles here. He changed shape, made himself long and thin like an eel, then disappeared into the cave. She morphed and followed him.

When she came out on the other side, her heart was racing. Glibber was something that really scared her, plus the sudden changes in pace and direction. The feeling of a sticky, slimy substance on parts of her body was only gradually disappearing. "Fun?" "Fear fun", she replied. He took on human form for a moment, she did the same, they looked into each other's eyes. "Push your limits?" She looked at him for a while. But what did she risk? Just one escape or exit command ... "Yes." She shivered as he gently wrapped her body around her. "Care to yield?" "Yield," she said, and they were paired. He seemed to know his way as he swam through the tangle of rocks, sea grass forests and corals. She relaxed and looked at the landscape that shimmered in blue-green colors.

"Pass if you dare." She was suddenly back in control, watching him reshape into a ball and drop vertically into a suction. She did the same. "Level 4. Constraint zone." She was floating in the suction, but the space did not let her go yet. "Accept." She started to fall ...

The fall itself was unspectacular, but an instant later after her adrenaline level rose: as she drifted through the widening cave, she suddenly felt suction cups on her skin, five or six tentacles holding her back. "Morph", her companion signaled. She considered, then concentrated on an elongated shape with a smooth, moist surface. The grip of the tentacles weakened, the suction cups began to lose their hold on her skin, she was able to swim freely. Her heart was pounding. From the outside she looked like a seal now, but it was much easier to escape the tentacles now, out of the cave into a wide open area shimmering in blue and green. Her companion and two other men had resumed their human avatars, she did the same. She felt their eyes on her. In the distance, somewhat out of place, a single large flower stood on a stem that swayed gently in the water, the flower was lit up as if individual sun rays from above had found their way down here.

"Dare?" Her companion swam a little way towards the flower. She had no idea what to expect, but she followed him, turned on her back and slowly slid into the center of the basket. The feeling was overwhelming and unreal at the same time as the petals gently wrapped around her legs. Her companion and a second took her arms and put them behind her head, just as gently other petals wrapped around her wrists and forearms. Her pulse was going fast. The three morphed, suddenly long, thin, slippery bodies twisted around her limbs, slid around her neck and all over her defenseless body. Her heart started racing, she breathed quickly, but then she managed to overcome her fear. She let herself be driven by the waves of pure pleasure spreading in her body, orgasms flowed into each other, she lost all sense of time and place.

"Escape." She was instantly back on level 2. Her heart was still racing, her mouth was full of the salty taste that she actually detested. She floated in the water for a while, tried to calm down, felt what she had just experienced. "Did not like?" His concerned question came as a surprise, her companion was nearby. "Contrary", she replied. "Panicked." At some point, when the hot sperm poured into her mouth, it had become too much for her. "IC", he said. "Meet again?" "Perhaps", she replied, still too dazed to grasp a clear thought. "Exit."

Two minutes later she was safely on the floor again, the helmet was removed. No trace of sperm in her mouth, only her own wetness between the legs was still present. "Come on, we'll help you get out of your suit."

Twenty minutes later, the chubby lady in her mid thirties was sitting in her sports convertible freshly showered in nightly Los Angeles. Another hour to Santa Monica if there was no traffic jam. Her open hair was floating in the wind.

Acquaintances

Sven: Hello big one, what's up?

Kim was pulled out of her half-sleep by the quiet "Plung" of the messenger service. It was already dark outside, and somewhat cooler air came through the open window into her tiny student room in Barcelona, where the blonde, light-skinned Norwegian had been studying Spanish for two years. More of Spanish life, if she was honest. She might be 22 or 23 years old.

She picked up the tablet that lay on the bedside table. A smile crossed her lips.

Kim: Hello little one, hot here, how's it going on the island?

Sven was some two years younger than her. He had graduated from high school in mechanical engineering and then started working on one of the large oil platforms in the North Sea. His life was determined by the unchangeable schedule of duties: 14 days on the island, 30 days free. As far as she knew, he had only returned to work a few days ago.

Sven: Shift just over, freshly showered on the bed. Waves only 10 feet high. Not up to sleeping.

Kim: Showering pointless here, almost 40 centigrade. Not up to going out.

There was no answer for a while. She tried to imagine him, with his big lanky body, his frizzy brown hair, his gentle brown eyes. She missed him right now.

Sven: Talk? Video?

Kim considered. Because of the heat, she lay naked on her rumpled bed and didn't feel like getting up or at least getting dressed.

Kim: I am naked.

Sven: So what? Me too.

OK. She should have predicted. Sven was just Sven. She had to smile again, on the other hand, it did not matter. In the solitude of the rural area outside of Bergen it had been inevitable that they had come closer to each other over time. So it was between them, no big deal.

She checked the webcam, yes, it was still clipped above the large LCD screen, which took up almost the entire wall at the foot of the bed.

Kim: Wait, I'll get something to drink.

Sven: Good idea.

Two minutes later she was back on the bed with an ice-cold can of beer from her tiny fridge. She ran her hand quickly through her hair, adjusted the preview so that only her face and small breasts could be seen, and pressed the video button.

"Hey little one", she simply spoke into the room. It took a while for his picture to appear on the large display. "Hey big one."

As she hadn't expected otherwise, he showed a total body shot. The camera was intentionally mounted so low that his cock appeared huge compared to the face due to the parallax effect. It was already half-erect.

"Do you think I still don't know what it looks like?"

Grin. "Maybe you've already forgotten if you never go out?"

He zoomed in a little, she could see his boyish smile better now. "Cheers, big one." He took a large sip from his beer can.

"Cheers little one." She popped the can and drank as well.

"You can't forget it anyway. How many men are on the island? 500?"

"400 is enough. And 20 women. But we don't shower together."

"Regrettably as far as women are concerned. With this kind of equipment." She smiled.

"Thank you, but this does not work out. It is frowned upon by the management. Only sometimes there are two or three hookers here for a few days."

"Really? Why only sometimes?"

"Aviation weather. With a wind force of nine, they gratefully refrain."

"And nothing for you?"

"No, besides, you know I'm not into rubbers."

"Rubbers, what for?" The HIV vaccination had been around for a few years now.

"Company policy. The company wants to get rid of the hookers completely, the works council insists, but rubbers are in the 50-year-old works agreement, which can therefore not be changed. Luckily this doesn't apply to you, big one."

"And what do I get from it? My affair has already left for Connecticut, and it's so hot here ..."

"Yes, you should have studied Icelandic instead of Spanish. You would have found an American there too."

"Thanks for your kind advice. It's helping me a lot right now, little one."

He zoomed out again and focused on his already erect penis. "You'd need something like this."

"How can you stand having such a one-track mind", she returned snappily. But she had to secretly admit that he was not entirely wrong. But why did she talk to him on the phone in first place, it had been predictable that she would get horny.

"Then what are you thinking about?", the well-deserved answer came in. Fuck, fucking, of course, what else. "Now is not always." Not very convincing, she had to admit to herself.

"With which you admitted that you do now", he etched. "Already damp in that little pink slit of yours?"

She watched as his hand slowly grip his now fully erect penis. "Now at least wait", she hissed at him.

"What exactly for, big one?", he returned sweetly. "Isn't it too hot or did I get that wrong?"

"Fuck you." The words were spoken quickly, but just as quickly his reaction came in the form of slow, provocative wanking movements. "Now wait. It wasn't meant that way."

He didn't stop masturbating. "Can you keep looking away until you find your big black rubber prick in your mess?"

In response, she stuck out her tongue and then demonstratively put two fingers of her right hand between her lips. "A real woman does not need it any more than you, little one."

"Well then let me see." But she already had reached for the tablet computer and adjusted perspective. Yes, that would be awesome. OK. She put the tablet out of her hand, stretched out comfortably, spread her legs wide and let the two wet fingers slowly slide over her labia.

He slowed down until he was in sync with her. "Well, what do we want to think about together?"

"Bjorn and Inga, Midsommar?", she asked. She took one of her already stiff nipples in her hand and pushed the two wet fingers of the other deep into her vagina.

"Hot, yes", he said. "Now each for ourselves and then ... you know ..."

But she had already slipped into her own world. A little unfocused, she looked at the big picture of the slowly wanking cock, while she versedly got herself going. Other images flashed into her mind as her thoughts traced that evening on the farm over a year ago.

He was holding back. He knew Kim very well, he knew she would take her time before she would allow herself going off. So while watching her, he was concerned with pushing himself to the limit again and again, easing slightly, maintaining tension. It would come to her pretty suddenly, he was prepared.

"Three", finally sounded from the speaker. "Two", he replied. "One and ..." "... now", both exclaimed at the same time.

"Kinky, absolutely kinky", she said as she put her soaking fingers to her mouth and stuck her tongue out. "You too?"

She watched him collect the incredible amounts of sperm from his cock and belly. He also put his fingers to his mouth. "Of course."

There was a long silence, suddenly the video connection was interrupted.

Sven: Kiss and thanks, sweetie. I will sleep well now.

Kim: Kiss and thanks, I hope I will too.

With a large sip, she emptied the rest of the beer out of the can.

Sven: Again? When?

Kim: Un-ask this question, little one.

Sven: OK until sometime, big one. CU.

Kim: CU.